Cars

Rushing! HONKING! Zooming!

by Patricia Hubbell

illustrated by Megan Halsey
and Sean Addy

Marshall Cavendish Children

Text copyright © 2006 by Patricia Hubbell
Illustrations copyright © 2006 by Megan Halsey and Sean Addy
First Marshall Cavendish paperback edition, 2010

Marshall Cavendish Corporation
99 White Plains Road, Tarrytown, NY 10591
www.marshallcavendish.us/kids

Library of Congress Cataloging-in-Publication Data
Hubbell, Patricia.
Cars : rushing! honking! zooming! / by Patricia Hubbell ;
illustrated by Megan Halsey and Sean Addy.
p. cm.
Summary: Illustrations and rhyming text celebrate different kinds of cars
and what they can do.
978-0-7614-5296-6 (hardcover)
978-0-7614-5616-2 (paperback)
[1. Automobiles—Fiction. 2. Stories in rhyme.] I. Halsey, Megan, ill.
II. Addy, Sean, ill. III. Title.
PZ8.3.H848Car 2006
[E]—dc22
2005027071

The illustrations are rendered in clip art,
etchings, original drawings, and maps.

Book design by Virginia Pope
Editor: Margery Cuyler
Printed in Malaysia (T)

1 3 5 6 4 2

mc Marshall Cavendish
Children

For my favorite kids who ride
in the backseat—Lil and Zak
—M.H.

To Mom, Helma, Mary, and Anna
and all the roads traveled
—S.A.

Start the motor! Turn the key!
Compact car or SUV.

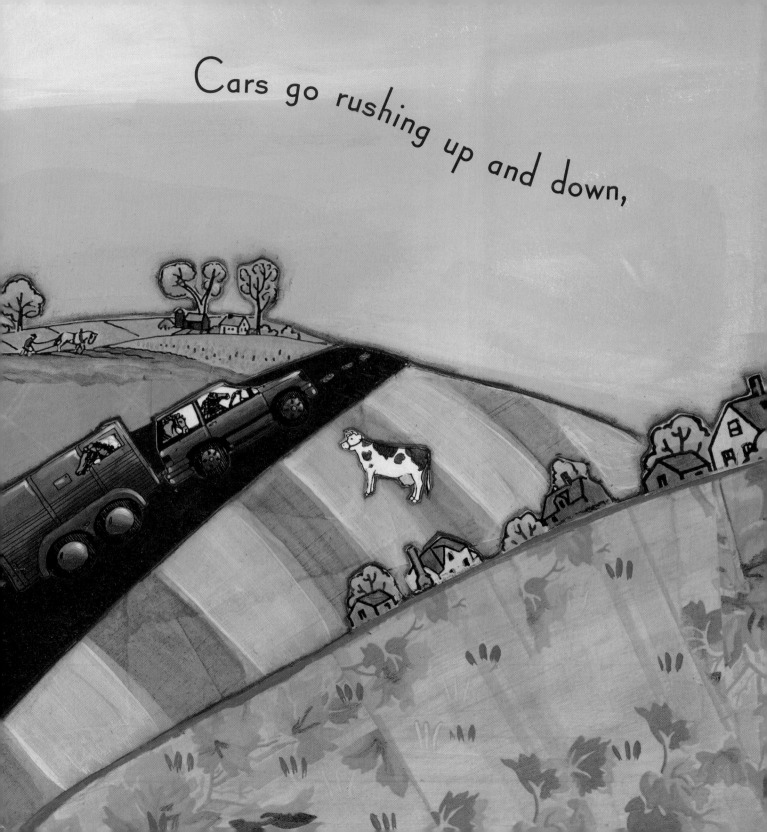

Cars go rushing up and down,

Convertibles and limousines

packed with waving,
giggling teens.

Taxis swerving, dodging, beeping.

Families hailing, shouting, leaping.

Police cars darting, passing, dashing.
Sirens wailing.
Bright lights flashing.

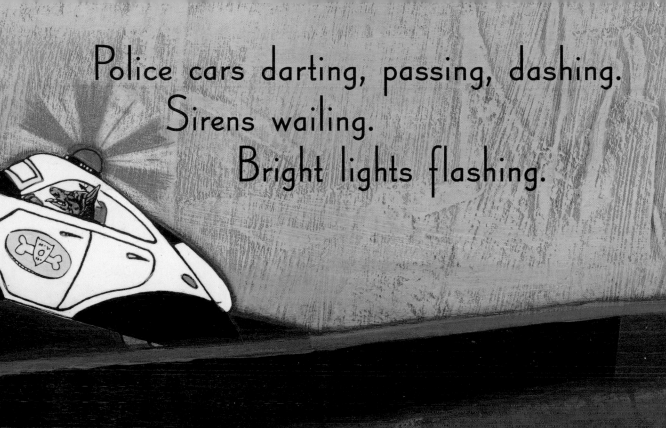

Fire chief's car, bright shiny red.

Hook and ladder up ahead.

WE LEAD
IN
QUALITY
and
SERVICE

Cars with two doors. Cars with four.
Cars with stick shifts on the floor.

Cars with horns that toot and blare.
Cars that big dogs like to share.

Race cars roaring 'round a track,

numbers painted on their back.

Hot rods.

Station wagons.

Vans.

Jeeps.

Delivery cars.

Pizza!!

Sedans.

Racing! Rushing! Honking! Squealing! Stopping! Starting! Turning! Wheeling!

Garages where mechanics work

fixing cars that stall or jerk.

Greasing axles. Checking tires.
Engine. Carburetor. Wires.

Light

Axle

Tire

Muffler

Radiator. Muffler. Lights.

Carburetor

Engine

Wires

Radiator

Everything must be just right.

Add some oil.
Pump some gas.

Clean the
windshield's dirty glass.

Fasten seatbelts. Off we go!
Fast! Fast! Slow . . . Slow.
Whizzing here. Cruising there.
Cars can take us anywhere.

Mountain.

Desert.

Farmland.

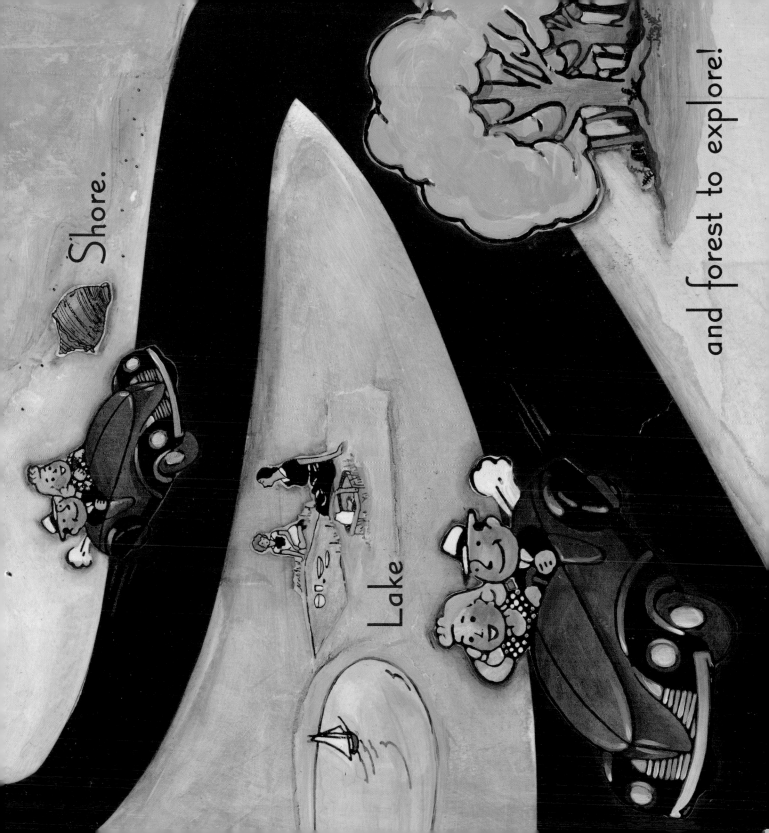

Shore.

Lake

and forest to explore!

Park your toy cars in a row.
Pick one out and—off you go!

Make a road around your room.
Zip! Turn! **STOP!** Zoom!

Cars go
North,
South,
East,
and
West.

They do their jobs . . .

. . . and then they rest.